It's the First Day of Preschool,

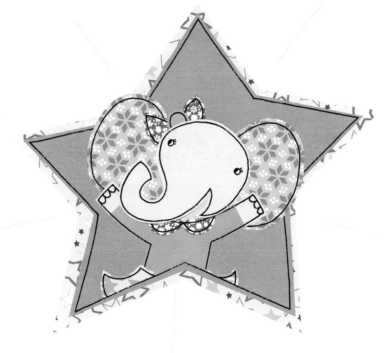

Jane Smith

Albert Whitman & Company
Chicago, Illinois

It's the first day of preschool!

Preschool is a place to have lots of fun and learn new things.

My mommy and daddy told me
I will meet a teacher, sing songs,

read stories, play,

paint pictures, and
make new friends.

That sounds like fun! But I really like playing at home with my mommy and my little sister and my Princess Kitty doll and all my toys.

"What if I don't make any friends?" I ask Mommy.
"Don't worry, Chloe Zoe. All the other kids want to
make new friends too, just like you. Look for a smiling
face and say hello!"

In the morning, I pack a special snack and my Princess Kitty doll in my hearts-and-stars backpack. My tummy feels flip-floppy nervous and flip-floppy excited. I am ready to sing, read, play, paint, and make new friends!

When we get to my preschool, my family walks me to my classroom and then it's time to say good-bye. Suddenly I don't want my mommy and daddy to leave me!

I peek into the classroom. It looks big and loud and busy. There are a lot of kids. Maybe one of them could be my friend.

Then a tall boy bumps into me
as he runs through the door.
"Hey!" I say, frowning.
"Oops! Sorry!" he calls out.

Teacher Amy comes over. She holds my
hand, and I try really hard not to cry.

"Don't worry!" Teacher Amy smiles.
"Come with me!" I wave good-bye to
my mommy and daddy and go inside
the classroom.

Teacher Amy gives me my very own cubby for my things.
It has my name, CHLOE ZOE, already on it! I give Princess
Kitty a quick hug for luck before tucking her away.

Teacher Amy gathers everyone for circle time. I don't see anyone I know so I want to sit by Teacher Amy.

But twin girls in matching pink dresses are faster than me! They sit down on either side of the teacher so I have to find another spot.

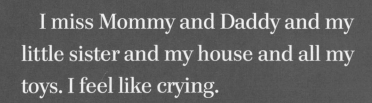

I miss Mommy and Daddy and my little sister and my house and all my toys. I feel like crying.

But then another girl smiles
at me! My heart skips a beat
and I smile back.

Everyone sings the "Good Morning" song and introduces themselves. The girl who smiled at me says her name is Mary Margaret. The boy sitting next to me is Ben.

Teacher Amy hands out special instruments for music time. I really want to play the tambourine, but I get a pink drum instead. Tears bubble up again.

"Hi! Will you trade with me?" asks Mary Margaret.

"Pink is my favorite color."

"Oh! Sure!" I say.

"Great!" Mary Margaret smiles at me again.

Together the whole class sings "Old MacDonald Had a Farm" while we tap out the beat on our instruments.

Everyone takes turns picking animals for Old MacDonald's farm. I pick a chicken! "With a cluck, cluck here and a cluck, cluck there…" we sing.

For snack time, I want to sit with Mary Margaret, but she's already sitting with George, the tall boy who bumped into me. I'm not sure if I should join them.

Mary Margaret calls me over and waves. So I sit with her and George. I smile really big and say, "Hello!"

"Hi!" George says. "Do want to share my orange?"

"Wow! Sure! I love oranges," I say. That is super nice. I think I made two new friends today!

At the playground, Mary Margaret, George, and I play in the sandbox. We build a giant sand castle using all the toys—buckets, shovels, rakes, and molds!

During arts-and-crafts time, we each get our own easel and paint set. Mary Margaret paints a pretty butterfly and George paints a robot. I paint a picture for Mommy and Daddy of the sand castle we built.

At the end of the day, everyone gathers their backpacks, coats, and artwork and sits down in a circle again. We sing the "Good-Bye" song to all our new friends.

When my mommy and daddy arrive to pick me up, I tell them I can't wait to play with Mary Margaret and George again tomorrow! Preschool *is* fun!

For more Chloe Zoe fun
—like crafts, coloring pages, games, and activities—
visit www.albertwhitman.com.

For Melanie, who loved pink as much as Mary Margaret

Also available:
It's Valentine's Day, Chloe Zoe!
It's Easter, Chloe Zoe!
It's the First Day of Kindergarten, Chloe Zoe!

More Chloe Zoe books coming soon:
It's Halloween, Chloe Zoe!
It's Thanksgiving, Chloe Zoe!

Library of Congress Cataloging-in-Publication data is on file with the publisher.

Text and pictures copyright © 2016 by Jane Smith
Published in 2016 by Albert Whitman & Company
ISBN 978-0-8075-2456-5
Printed in China
10 9 8 7 6 5 4 3 2 1 HH 24 23 22 21 20 19 18 17 16

Design by Jordan Kost

For more information about Albert Whitman & Company,
visit our web site at www.albertwhitman.com.